The
Interceptor
Pilot

By the same author

Olt
Lydia
Corroboree
The Volcanoes from Puebla

In the jungle the wreckage
of an aircraft has been found.
Clothed in the tatters of a
uniform, a skeleton sits at
the controls, the skull resting
on the collarbone, as though
lost in meditaion.

Evan S. Connnell

The Interceptor Pilot

Kenneth Gangemi

Marion Boyars
London · Boston

Published in Great Britain
and the United States in 1980
by Marion Boyars Publishers Ltd.
18 Brewer Street, London W1R 4AS
and Marion Boyars Publishers Inc.
99 Main Street, Salem, New Hampshire 03079

Australian distribution by Thomas C. Lothian
4–12 Tattersalls Lane, Melbourne, Victoria 3000

© Kenneth Gangemi 1980

Library of Congress Cataloging in Publication Data

Gangemi, Kenneth, 1937–
    The interceptor pilot.

    I. Title.
PZ4.G1925In (PS3557.A5)   813′.54   79–56849
ISBN 0–7145–2699–1

PART
ONE

1

The beginning of the film is set at a Naval Air Station somewhere in the western United States. It could be any one of the southwestern or Rocky Mountain states: Arizona, New Mexico, Utah, Nevada, Colorado, Idaho, Wyoming, or Montana. The reason is mainly cinematic. The film will be in color, and the setting might as well be one of great natural beauty. It will be a western landscape of sagebrush and semi-desert plains and striking mountains.

The opening shot is of long grass blowing in the breeze at the edge of a concrete runway. The camera holds on this opening shot and then slowly begins to rise until distant mountains are seen in the background. Cut to a shot down one of the taxiways: we see a taxiing plane, still far in the distance, as it slowly approaches. The image of the plane shimmers above the sun-heated runway.

At this point the titles begin to appear on the screen. The camera holds on the shot of the taxiing plane, providing background for the titles, and the plane steadily grows in size. The sound of the jet engine gradually becomes louder. By the time the titles are completed, the taxiing plane has approached to within fifty feet of the camera.

AUGUST 1966 is superimposed on the screen, and

then the camera cuts to a side view of the plane. Aviation enthusiasts will recognize it to be an early version of the F-8 Crusader, a jet fighter widely used in reserve squadrons. Painted on the plane is the word NAVY in big letters, the number of the reserve squadron, and the name of the Naval Air Station.

Cut to a shot of the pilot in the cockpit. The visor of his flight helmet is down and obscures most of his face. Cut to a closeup of the microphone touching his lips as he speaks to the control tower. We hear the standard radio exchange with the tower as he obtains clearance for takeoff.

The opening sequence in the film shows the takeoff in the F-8 and the initial climb to about 10,000 feet. Several shots from the cockpit show the pilot calmly looking down at the mountains and the semi-desert landscape below. The camera then cuts to a closeup of a blinking emergency light: FUEL PRESSURE. There is a quick closeup of the power indicator beginning to fall off.

The pilot immediately declares an emergency. We listen to the rapid exchange over the radio with the control tower. Cut to quick shots of the man in the tower as he speaks into the microphone. Cut back to the pilot as he goes through various procedures in the cockpit. The camera shows the maneuverings of the F-8 as the pilot turns back to the field for a straight-in approach. We observe as he brings the plane in for a fine emergency landing.

Cut to the scene at the end of the runway. Fire trucks and emergency vehicles drive up to the plane as it comes to a stop. Cut to the pilot in the cockpit as he opens the canopy. He removes his flight helmet and we see his face for the first time. The pilot unhitches his shoulder harness, climbs down from the cockpit, and talks briefly with several of the men. After a few minutes he gets into a jeep to be driven back to Flight Operations.

Cut to a shot of the man who is behind the wheel of the jeep. As he drives away from the plane he compliments the pilot on his handling of the emergency. The pilot smiles and nods his head. He briefly describes what happened and then mentions that some of the F-8s are getting old. He speaks with the casual manner of an experienced pilot who has made a number of emergency landings.

The two men talk as the jeep bumps across the airfield. The driver asks several questions, and we learn that the pilot is a reservist who is completing his two-week summer training. We learn that the flight in the F-8 was his last flight.

The camera cuts to an aerial view of the jeep in the middle of the airfield. We can see the layout of the runways and the mountains rising in the distance. Cut back to the pilot inside the jeep. The bright-colored squadron patch is visible on his shoulder. The camera moves in to a closeup of his face, and we see that he looks as though he is in his late thirties. Cut to a closeup of the leather name tag on his flight suit: JAMES J. WILSON/LIEUTENANT COMMANDER/USNR.

2

Two hours later. The scene is the office of a Navy doctor. Wilson has just completed a physical examination and is buttoning up his shirt. The doctor is sitting at his desk, filling out the medical form. Cut to a closeup of the doctor as he writes. He tells Wilson that he is in good shape for a man who is thirty-eight years old. He tells him that his reflexes are excellent and that his vision is still 20/20.

The doctor has Wilson's file, which contains his military record and medical history, in front of him on the desk. Cut to a closeup of the file as he picks it up. He has already read it over, and it is evident that he finds it interesting. The doctor asks several questions. We learn that Wilson was a fighter pilot during the Korean War and was wounded in action. We learn that he flew eighty-four missions and was credited with shooting down five MIGs.

3

One hour later. The scene is a busy office in the Administration Building at the Naval Air Station. Wilson is standing at a counter. We hear voices in the background and also a mixture of office sounds: electric typewriters, telephones ringing, file cabinets closing.

Cut to a closeup of military discharge papers. We see the name James J. Wilson neatly typed at the top, and also the date: 14 August 1966. Cut back to Wilson. He is talking with an enlisted man on the other side of the counter, and the discharge papers are between them. We listen to their conversation and learn that Wilson has resigned from the Naval Reserve.

The camera shows Wilson as he takes the discharge papers, folds them carefully, and puts them into his pocket. He picks up the suitcase by his feet. Tracking shot as he walks down the corridor and out of the Administration Building and emerges into bright sunshine. He walks along a sidewalk and then crosses over to a parking lot. We can see the distant mountains in the background.

Wilson stops at a late-model station wagon, and the camera cuts to a closeup of a section of the windshield. We see a parking sticker that says UNIVERSITY OF COLORADO/FACULTY. Wilson unlocks the station wagon, puts his suitcase into the back, and gets behind the wheel. Cut to a closeup of his hand as he turns the keys in the ignition. Closeup of his face as he puts on sunglasses. He backs the station wagon out, leaves the parking lot, and drives slowly down the narrow street of the Naval Air Station.

Cut to a shot of a construction site ahead. The street is being torn up for a pipeline, and one of the construction workers is positioning a jackhammer. There is a quick closeup of the chalk-marked asphalt. Cut to the construction worker as he positions the jackhammer and begins to lean on it.

The camera cuts to a shot of the station wagon as it slowly approaches the construction site. We begin to hear the chattering sound of the jackhammer. Cut to a closeup of Wilson as he drives. The sound of the jack-hammer becomes louder, and the camera moves in to a closeup of his sunglasses.

As the camera holds on this closeup, the sound of the jackhammer is heard to change to a similar sound: the hammering noise of 20mm aerial cannon. The first flash-back begins as the closeup of the sunglasses dissolves to one of Wilson's memories from the Korean War.

Dissolve to gun-camera footage of one of the classic shots of aerial combat. A North Korean MIG-15 is shown as it veers off to one side, a stream of tracer bullets pouring into it from Wilson's 20mm aerial cannon. The horizon appears to tilt in the background at a steep angle. The MIG-15 continues to receive fire for several seconds, and we continue to hear the hammering noise of the aerial cannon. Then black smoke begins to appear, the plane veers sharply, and it suddenly explodes.

The flashback ends and the camera dissolves back to

the closeup of Wilson's sunglasses. Cut to a shot of the construction site: the station wagon has passed it, and the man operating the jackhammer appears to recede into the distance. The sound of the jackhammer diminishes until it is no longer heard.

The camera shows Wilson as he continues to drive through the Naval Air Station. Shots of the station wagon as it proceeds are intercut with shots of Wilson behind the wheel. He drives past various buildings, past a flight line of F-8s, and finally drives up to the sentry gate.

Cut to a shot of the two Marines on duty as they salute. Wilson returns the salute and passes through. The camera shows the two Marines as they look after the departing station wagon, and then rises to show the sign mounted above the sentry gate. The sign contains the name of the Naval Air Station, the town in which it is located, and the state.

Cut back to Wilson behind the wheel of the station wagon. He accelerates on a straight road in semi-desert country. It is evident that he has a long drive ahead. Wilson settles back, adjusts his sunglasses, and puts on the radio. There is a quick closeup of his hand turning the knob with a *click*. We listen to music for a few seconds, and then the music is interrupted for a bulletin about Vietnam.

4

Six weeks later. The University of Colorado. The reason
for the choice of this particular university is mainly cinematic. It really could be any one of the state universities
in the West. The University of Colorado, however, has
an attractive campus that will photograph well. It also
has striking mountains to the west that will show up
nicely in some of the distance shots.

The fall semester has begun and Wilson has resumed
his classes. The sequence opens with a montage of various shots of campus activity. It is almost noontime and
the campus is bustling with students. The camera eventually rises to a third-story window of one of the buildings. It moves in until we see that a class is in progress.

Cut to a shot of Wilson as he stands at the blackboard. He is explaining a diagram that depicts the fuselage and swept wings of a jet aircraft. Wilson draws lines
from the nose back towards the wings. He explains that
the lines represent the shock waves that are generated
when the aircraft is traveling near the speed of sound.
We listen as Wilson continues to lecture. For a few
seconds we all learn something about the reasons for
swept wings on jet aircraft.

Cut to a shot of the students in the classroom as they
listen attentively. The course is Introduction to Aero-
nautical Engineering, a survey course for students in

other engineering disciplines. Wilson is apparently well-regarded by the students, for the classroom is filled. He lectures with the ease that comes from many years of experience.

Cut back to the blackboard. Wilson begins to write a complicated equation beside the diagram. We hear the rapid tapping of the chalk. As he writes the equation he explains it with a ten-second burst of mathematical terminology.

Cut to the students in the classroom: they hurry to copy the equation in their notes. Cut back to Wilson as he finishes his explanation and replaces the chalk on the blackboard. Closeup of his face as he calmly looks out at the classroom and waits for the students to finish copying the equation.

The bell rings and the class is over. We begin to hear the usual between-classes noise from the hallways. Wilson picks up the open textbook and gives the assignment for the next meeting. Then he pauses for a moment, looks out at the students, and casually delivers a very funny joke. Cut to a shot of the filled classroom and all the students laughing.

5

Twenty minutes later. The scene is the enormous cafeteria in the Student Union. It is 12:30 p.m. and the cafeteria is very crowded. We hear a mixture of sounds: music, cafeteria noises, hundreds of conversations. The sequence opens with a montage of various shots. We see groups of students at tables, cafeteria employees dishing up food, the cashiers at the cash registers, students coming off the line with trays.

Cut to a shot of Wilson on the cafeteria line, talking with another man. They have food on their trays and are waiting for the line to move. We see that the other man is about Wilson's age. It is evident that he is also a member of the faculty. His appearance indicates that his field is in one of the humanities, possibly English or history.

We will see that Wilson and the other professor, whose name is Miller, are good friends who often have lunch together. Professor Miller is one of the minor characters in the film. He will be seen as a leftist, but one who is more genial than militant. He will be portrayed quite favorably.

The camera moves in towards the two men and their conversation begins to be heard. They are talking politics, as they often do, and have resumed an old debate.

16

We will see that Professor Miller is further to the left than Wilson.

Cut to a shot of Miller as he looks at Wilson and says, 'What have you decided about Korea?' Cut to Wilson. He tells Miller that he hasn't decided anything. Cut back to Miller as he smiles and says, 'Well, it's perfectly clear to *me*.'

Professor Miller than delivers a brief historical interpretation of the Korean conflict. It is essentially the Soviet view. When he has finished, the camera cuts to Wilson. He shakes his head and says, 'I don't think it's that simple.' He looks at Miller. 'I'm still not sure about Korea. But I'm *convinced* about Vietnam.'

The cafeteria line begins to move, and the two men continue to talk as they slide their trays along the rails. They reach the cash register, pay the cashier, and pick up their trays. Tracking shot as they walk a zig-zag route through the tables of the crowded cafeteria.

The two men sit down and begin their lunch. There is some idle conversation at first, a little faculty gossip, a few exchanges about their wives and children. Professor Miller happens to mention the crash of a small airplane that was in the newspaper. Wilson says that he read about it. Miller asks him what could have caused it, and Wilson tells him it was probably pilot error.

Cut to a shot of Professor Miller as he is reminded of something. He opens his attaché case and pulls out tabloid newspaper. A quick closeup of the masthead shows it to be the *National Guardian* or a similar leftist publication. Miller opens the newspaper to a photograph. He folds the newspaper and pushes it across the table to Wilson. Cut to a closeup of the photograph: it shows a hospital in North Vietnam that was bombed by American planes.

Miller says, 'I know you think as little of this kind of thing as I do, but can you tell me *why?*' Cut to a closeup of Wilson as he looks at the photograph. After a few seconds he says, 'I don't know. It might have been faulty intelligence. Possibly the briefing officer told the pilots about hospital crosses being painted on ammunition dumps.' He looks up at Miller and says, 'It was simply a mistake, the kind of terrible mistake that is inevitable in any war.'

The two men finish their lunch and get up from the table. The camera follows them as they walk through the cafeteria and the lobby of the Student Union. We listen to their conversation, which has shifted to a more cheerful subject: the faculty tennis matches, where they are entered as a doubles team. They emerge from the building into bright sunshine. Tracking shot of the two men talking together as they leisurely cross the green campus.

6

Two nights later. Cut to a shot of a late-model Porsche as it drives down a suburban street. The camera shows the car as it slows, turns into a driveway, and comes to a stop. The headlights are turned off. The door of the Porsche is opened a crack, causing the interior to be lighted, and the camera cuts to a shot of the driver. We see that it is Professor Miller.

The camera follows Miller as he gets out of the car and walks across the lawn to the lighted house. He rings the bell – there is a quick closeup of his finger pushing the button – and waits for a few seconds. Cut to a shot of an attractive young woman as she opens the door. She smiles at Professor Miller and he steps inside.

There is the usual exchange of greetings and small talk. We learn that the woman's name is Helen and that she is Wilson's wife. We also learn that Wilson is in Denver and will not be home until late. Helen takes Miller's coat and they go into the living room. Cocktails are mixed and they continue to talk.

After a few minutes Helen tells Professor Miller the reason she asked him to come over. We learn that she is quite worried about her husband. She tells Miller that he has been acting in a strange manner. He seems to be preoccupied with something, and she has no idea what it is. Helen asks Miller if he has noticed anything. Miller thinks for a few seconds and then says that lately Wilson has been talking a lot about Vietnam.

Helen seems to be satisfied to hear this. She then asks Miller if he has ever seen her husband's books on Korea. Miller looks somewhat surprised and says that he has not. She asks him to come with her, and the two of them get up. The camera follows them as they walk through the house and into Wilson's library.

Cut to a shot of Professor Miller as he stands in front of a section of the bookshelves. He is obviously impressed by the quantity of material. Besides the many books on Korea, there are stacks of files of clippings. It is all evidence of years of study. He asks Helen how long it has been since Wilson flew in Korea. She tells him it has been over thirteen years.

Helen moves to another part of the library that contains memorabilia from Wilson's flying days. She tells Miller that her husband wanted to be a pilot ever since he was a boy. She brings out a childhood scrapbook, and the camera cuts to closeups of the pages as they are turned. There are photographs of fighter planes from both World Wars. There are photographs of famous aces – German, French, British, American – standing by their planes.

Helen puts the childhood scrapbook down, picks up more recent memorabilia, and shows it to Professor Miller. The camera cuts to another series of closeups. We see a group photograph of Wilson with his classmates in flight school; a photograph of Wilson beside his Navy trainer after his first solo; a photograph of him receiving his wings.

Helen shows Professor Miller some newspaper clippings. There is one for every time Wilson downed a MIG in Korea. The camera cuts to closeups of the clippings as Miller looks at them. Helen then shows him the Navy document that named Wilson an ace after he had a total of five MIGs.

She mentions the nightmares her husband had after Korea. 'He would never tell me about them, but sometimes he would talk in his sleep. He would wake up in the middle of the night and he would be saying something about a school. It was always something about a school.' She tells Miller that her husband underwent psychiatric treatment. The nightmares became less frequent and eventually stopped.

Helen takes another newspaper clipping and shows it to Professor Miller. 'He was all right for years, but then *this* started him off. Now he has those nightmares almost every night.' Cut to a shot of the clipping. It is the headlined story that announces the escalation of the war, the bombing of North Vietnam. Miller takes the clipping and looks at it. Cut from his face to a closeup of the headline: JOHNSON ORDERS BOMBING OF NORTH VIETNAM.

7

Two weeks later. The scene is the language laboratory at the University of Colorado. We see a man with his back to the camera as he sits at one of the audio desks. A language record is revolving on the turntable. The man is wearing earphones and is evidently concentrating on the language lesson.

The camera cuts to a closeup of the revolving record, and we begin to hear it: the voices of a man and a woman as they converse in French. We listen to the conversation for about ten seconds and then the record ends. The man shuts off the turntable, removes his earphones, and stands up. We see that it is Wilson.

The camera shows him as he picks up the record, slips it into the jacket, and then pauses to look out across the room. Cut to a shot of the scene in the language laboratory: we see dozens of students sitting with earphones at the audio desks. Cut back to Wilson as he walks across the room. He reaches the desk and hands the French record to a pretty student. Closeups of their faces as they exchange smiles.

Cut to a shot of Professor Miller as he appears at the desk. 'Are you going to Paris this year?' he asks. Cut back to Wilson: we can see that he is surprised, but he quickly regains himself. He says hello to Miller, and the two men go out to the hallway to talk.

Professor Miller is curious about the French record and asks Wilson about it. Wilson replies that he is merely brushing up on his high school French. The conversation turns to other matters, and we learn that they have not seen each other for a while. It soon becomes evident that their relationship has changed.

Professor Miller presumes Wilson is busy and asks him what he is up to. Wilson is evasive and seems to resent the question. The bell suddenly rings. We hear doors opening and the beginning of the usual between-classes noise. Wilson looks at his watch, mentions a class coming up, and hurries off. Hold on a shot of Miller as he watches him walking down the hallway.

8

Two nights later. Cut to a shot of the house where Wilson and his family live. We recognize the house from the earlier scene when Professor Miller arrived to talk with Helen. It is now late at night and all the lights are out except for one on the ground floor. The camera begins to move in towards the house.

Cut to a shot of Wilson sitting in a comfortable chair in his living room. He is wearing a sportcoat and tie. A suitcase is standing by his chair, and a raincoat is thrown over it. We see that Wilson is just quietly sitting there, looking out over the living room. He is obviously thinking about many things.

An almost-finished drink is on the table beside his chair. Wilson reaches for the drink, finishes it, and replaces the glass on the table. He appears to be calm and relaxed. He is evidently satisfied that no one discovered his extensive preparations, and that he is at last ready to leave.

Wilson reaches inside his sportcoat. Cut to a closeup of his hand as he pulls out an airline ticket. The camera holds on the ticket jacket for a moment, and we see the trademark and name of the airline. Wilson opens the jacket to the ticket inside and looks at it. Cut to a closeup of the ticket: we see that it is a night flight from Denver to New York.

Cut back to Wilson as he looks at his watch and then replaces the ticket inside his sportcoat. He gets to his feet, picks up his raincoat and suitcase, and starts to walk towards the door. The camera follows him as he walks away. When he has turned the corner, the camera cuts back to a shot of the table. It moves in to a closeup of a white envelope that lies in the light of the lamp. We see the single handwritten word *Helen*.

PART
TWO

1

New York, two days later. Cut to a shot of the front of a subway train – the Lexington Avenue Express – as it emerges from the dark tunnel into the lighted station. We hear the sound of the train approaching, the sudden roar as it emerges from the tunnel, and then the sound of the brakes. Cut to a shot of people waiting on the crowded platform, and then to a quick closeup of one of the station signs: WALL STREET.

Cut to a shot of Wilson standing inside one of the subway cars. He is dressed in a business suit and is carrying his raincoat and a briefcase. The train comes to a stop, the doors open, and Wilson exits with a number of people. The camera follows him as he walks through the crowded station.

Cut to a shot of the sidewalk above: we see the subway exit and people coming up the stairs. Wilson is quickly spotted among them. Tracking shot of Wilson as he begins to make his way along the sidewalk. It is near lunchtime and the financial district is crowded.

The tracking shot of Wilson as he walks is intercut with shots of people and scenes that he passes, to give the sense of place, the feeling of New York. We see quick shots of men selling newspapers; businessmen getting out of taxis; office workers crowding into luncheonettes; men selling hot dogs from pushcarts; bankers and stockbrokers sitting in the backs of limousines.

Cut to a closeup of the street sign at Broadway and Wall Street. The camera shows Wilson as he looks up at it and then proceeds to cross the street. Cut to a shot of a pretty girl in a miniskirt as she begins to cross from the other side. The camera holds on her for a few seconds as she walks. Cut back to Wilson. Closeup of his face as he looks at the approaching girl.

2

One hour later. The thirty-seventh floor of an office building near Broadway and Wall Street in the financial district. Cut to a shot of the impressive front door of a firm of investment lawyers. The lettering on the frosted glass lists the partners and gives the impression of an old and established firm.

Dissolve to a shot of one of the interior offices. It is spacious and comfortable and furnished in good masculine taste. It gives an impression of permanence and respectability. The camera moves around the office, and we see bookcases that contain leather-bound law volumes; a portrait of Franklin Delano Roosevelt on one wall, a portrait of John Fitzgerald Kennedy on another; an enormous window that offers a magnificent view of the city below.

Cut to a shot of Wilson as he sits in a comfortable armchair. He is sitting next to a large leather-topped desk in front of the window. Cut to a shot of the man behind the desk. We see that he is dignified and scholarly-looking and appears to be in his early sixties. He is impeccably dressed in a conservative business suit. It is so dark it is almost black. He is wearing a vest.

Wilson and the distinguished-looking lawyer are in the middle of a lengthy conference. We listen as the man asks Wilson a series of questions and takes notes on a pad. There is a quick closeup of his hand as he writes with a fountain pen on the lined paper. We hear the rapid scratching of the pen.

Cut to a closeup of the lawyer. He stops writing, looks up at Wilson, and quietly says, 'Now what about your knowledge of American aircraft?' Cut to a shot of Wilson. 'The latest plane I've flown is the F-8, which is more or less obsolescent now. The early versions are being phased out. I don't know the F-4. As a matter of fact I don't know anything after the F-8.

Cut back to the lawyer, who looks pleased and says, 'That will be in your favor. Is there anything else you know that they could charge you with?' Cut back to Wilson, who nods his head. 'Two missiles that are operational. I used the latest Sidewinder on the range this summer, and also the Sparrow III.'

We listen as they continue to talk about Wilson's knowledge of American aircraft and weapons systems. The two men are quite at ease with each other. It is evident that they have talked before, that this is not their first meeting. We hear references to long-distance telephone calls from Colorado, and to a meeting the previous day.

It also becomes evident that the man is no ordinary investment lawyer. The details of his background are not relevant to the film, but possibly he was an active Communist for several years during the thirties. He eventually left the party, but retained his sympathy for the Soviet Union. He also maintained some political contacts in Europe. The man now has a prosperous law practice. He lives in an affluent suburb, where he is a registered Democrat. His friends think of him as a liberal.

31

The lawyer finishes his questions and turns to other matters. He asks Wilson for his passport. Wilson takes it out of his pocket and hands it across the desk. The lawyer opens the passport and makes a note of something on the pad. Cut to a quick closeup of the open passport: we see the photograph of Wilson on one page. The lawyer finishes writing and hands the passport back. He also hands Wilson a slip of paper and says, 'This is the man you will contact in Paris.'

The lawyer then takes a document from a folder. He looks at it briefly and hands it across the desk without a word. Cut to a shot of Wilson as he recognizes it and picks up a pen. There is a quick closeup of his hand as he signs his name. Wilson finishes signing the document and looks at it with a sober expression. Cut to a closeup as it lies upon the desk. We see the title at the top in black letters: LAST WILL AND TESTAMENT.

3

Twenty-four hours later. The scene is the interior of an Air France jetliner. It is the tourist-class section and almost all the seats are filled. We hear the usual *hum* that is present in passenger aircraft, the murmur of many conversations, and then the voice of the captain over the intercom. He begins one of his periodic reports to the passengers. We learn that the plane is cruising at an altitude of 33,000 feet over the Atlantic Ocean.

Cut to a shot of a pretty stewardess as she makes her way down the aisle. The camera holds on her and then cuts to a shot of Wilson sitting in one of the seats. He is dressed in a sportcoat and tie and is watching the approaching stewardess. Cut back to the girl as she continues walking down the aisle and then spots Wilson ahead. Quick closeups of their faces as they exchange smiles.

The girl passes Wilson and briefly lays a hand on his shoulder. He smiles at that. The camera holds on him as we continue to hear the voice of the captain giving his report to the passengers. They are approaching the coast of France and will soon begin their descent. The weather in Paris is cloudy and the temperature is fifty-eight degrees.

Wilson relaxes in the comfortable seat, his head resting upon the headrest. The smile gradually fades from his face, and we see that he now seems to be deep in thought. He is no doubt thinking about what he has done, and what lies ahead. The camera holds on this closeup of Wilson for a long time. We hear the voice of the captain as he finishes his report in English and begins to give the same report in French.

4

Paris, two days later. The scene is the interior of a café on one of the boulevards. We hear a mixture of sounds: conversations in French, music from a jukebox, the sound of urban traffic. Cut to a shot of a gleaming expresso machine. We observe the quick-moving hands of a woman as she goes through the procedure of making a cup of expresso coffee.

The woman turns and places the little cup of expresso on the counter. The camera holds on the steaming coffee and then slowly rises to show the customer. Wilson is seen standing there in his raincoat. We hear a brief exchange of French as he digs in his pocket and pays for the coffee.

The camera holds on Wilson as he drinks from the little cup. We continue to hear a mixture of sounds: the conversations in French, the music from the jukebox, the sound of urban traffic. In the background people are entering and leaving through the doors of the café. Automobiles can be seen moving along the boulevard, and the sound of traffic increases every time the doors are opened.

The camera shows Wilson as he looks at his watch, finishes his coffee, and then leaves the café. Tracking shot as he begins to make his way along the sidewalk. It is near lunchtime and the boulevard is crowded. The tracking shot of Wilson as he walks is intercut with shots of people and scenes that he passes, to give the sense of place, the feeling of Paris.

At one point Wilson takes a slip of paper out of his pocket and looks at it, as though to check an address. He puts it back in his pocket and then turns off the boulevard into a side street. As he approaches a large building, the camera cuts to a sign above the entrance doors. The word *Ecole* in the sign tells us the building is a school.

The doors are suddenly opened and a double file of French schoolchildren begins to come down the steps. The camera holds on them for a few seconds and then cuts back to Wilson. We see that he has stopped walking and is staring at the children.

Cut to a closeup of his face. He seems to be slightly shaken as he stands and looks at the children. The camera moves in to a closeup of his eyes. The usual street-sounds diminish and we begin to hear the faint but increasing sound of a jet beginning a dive-bombing run.

The camera holds on the closeup of Wilson's staring eyes. The sound of the jet on the dive-bombing run steadily increases. When it has become quite loud, it is suddenly interrupted. We hear the sound of an automobile horn and then breaking glass.

Cut to a shot of the street. A minor collision has occurred, and the two Frenchmen are getting out of their cars and beginning to shout at each other. Cut back to Wilson. We see that he is looking towards the street now and has evidently been snapped away from his thoughts.

The two Frenchmen gesture and argue in front of their cars. Wilson watches for a few seconds and then turns his head and looks back towards the school. Cut to a shot of the last of the schoolchildren as they turn a corner and disappear from sight. Cut back to Wilson as he remembers his appointment. He checks his watch, takes one more look at the school, and then resumes walking.

5

Two hours later. The scene is an office somewhere in Paris. It is small and sparsely furnished. Cut to a closeup of the hands of a girl as she changes a reel in a tape recorder. She completes the change, presses a button, and the new reel begins to spin. Cut to a shot of the girl – she is young and pretty – as she stands and looks down at the tape recorder.

Cut to the scene in the office. We see Wilson sitting in a folding chair next to a cheap metal desk. The girl, who appears to be French, is standing by the tape recorder and is looking down at him. Sitting behind the desk is a stocky middle-aged man with glasses. We will soon see that he is a Russian intelligence agent.

Wilson and the man both have their jackets off and their shirtsleeves rolled up. It is a warm October afternoon in Paris. They both appear to be somewhat fatigued, and we get the impression that they have been talking for some time.

Cut to the Russian agent as he says, 'But we have some of our latest equipment in the MIG-21. How do we know you will not land at one of the American bases?' Cut to Wilson. It is his first meeting with the agent and it is not going well. 'Then take the equipment out! Take it all out! Put in something that is ten or fifteen years old. I can use it. I used it in Korea.'

6

Two weeks later. The scene is the same office, but this time rain is streaming down the windows. We see that Wilson, the French girl, and the Russian intelligence agent are all in different clothes. They are in approximately the same positions, and the tape recorder is operating as usual.

We will see that everything is being carefully checked out by the Russians. They are interested but extremely cautious. They must be absolutely certain that Wilson is not an American agent. The whole procedure is taking time.

The camera cuts to the Russian agent sitting behind the desk. He has a dossier in front of him and is asking Wilson a series of questions about his wife, his friends, and the university. Cut to Wilson as he answers each one. The Russians have done a thorough job, and Wilson is surprised at some of the questions. He appears to answer each one to the satisfaction of the agent.

The agent finishes his questions, closes the dossier, and puts it aside. He looks at Wilson and almost smiles. 'You have figured this out very carefully. Many of your suggestions are good ones, and we intend to use them. But the suspicion – let us say the sense of caution – of some of our people is still not satisfied.'

Cut to a closeup of Wilson. He has evidently come a

long way in understanding the Russians during the past two weeks. 'If you insist, if it is absolutely necessary, I'm willing to undergo lie-detector tests, sodium pentothal, any of that.' Cut back to the agent. He nods and says, 'I think that is what we will do. If the results are in your favor, then we can proceed. It will satisfy the military people somewhat, and make our position stronger.'

Cut to Wilson, who says, '*Our* position? You mean *my* position.' Cut back to the agent, who is again almost smiling for the first time in two weeks. 'No, *our* position. You see, I am already convinced. I do not think you are an American agent.' Cut to the French girl as she moves over and shuts off the tape recorder with a *click*.

7

The next morning. It is the final phase of the lengthy interrogation. The camera cuts to a shot of Wilson sitting in a chair. He is all set up with the lie detector and is answering questions.

Cut to the Russian agent as he reads the questions from a many-paged list. Cut back to Wilson as he answers each one. Closeups of his face as he answers the more important questions. We see that some of them are political.

The camera occasionally cuts to the French girl at the lie detector. She watches the apparatus carefully and makes small adjustments. There are closeups of the various dials and recording devices. Labels in French tell what is being measured: heartbeat, blood pressure, respiration rate, electrodermal response. We observe the fluctuations as Wilson answers the questions.

8

The afternoon of the same day. The camera shows Wilson lying on a couch with his sleeve rolled up. The tape recorder is operating and the Russian agent is standing by with the same list of questions.

Cut to a shot of the French girl as she gives Wilson an injection of sodium pentothal. Closeup of his arm as the needle goes in. Closeup of the level of the liquid as it moves down in the graduated syringe.

9

Moscow, one week later. The scene is a conference room somewhere in the Kremlin. The camera shows high-level officials of the Soviet Union, military and civilian, sitting around an enormous table. The familiar domes and spires of the Moscow skyline are visible through the windows. The usual portrait of Lenin is on the wall.

The camera cuts to closeups of the various men. It lingers on one of them, and we see that he is not a Russian like the others. He is rather small and has Oriental features. Insignia on his military uniform reveal him to be a representative of North Vietnam.

Cut to a closeup of a thick file on the conference table. We see Russian words written on it, and in smaller letters *James Wilson*. Cut to a photograph of Wilson as it is circulated around the table. Closeups of several of the men as they look at it.

It is evident that all the intelligence data is in, and the Russians have to make a decision. The conference begins, and we observe as two factions develop. One faction still does not trust Wilson. It also thinks the operation too risky for other reasons. The other faction thinks it is a great opportunity that must not be missed.

There are occasional shots of the representative from North Vietnam. But he is asked nothing and says nothing, he only listens. The conference goes on for a long time. We listen to the various men as they deliver their arguments.

'The American says he will fly only the latest MIG-21, he will not fly an earlier version. He says he is not going to North Vietnam to commit suicide. . . . This is not a military operation. We can send fifty pilots to North Vietnam in a matter of hours. This is a *propaganda* operation. . . . This man has received the Distinguished Flying Cross. He is a professor at an American university. . . . You cannot talk about what we have done in the past. There is no precedent for this. . . . What if he gets shot down the first time he goes up?. . . We *still* win. It is *still* a propaganda victory.'

10

Two days later. The scene is an office somewhere in Moscow. It is the office of a general in the Soviet Air Force. The camera shows a small meeting taking place. The faction favoring the use of Wilson has won, and the logistics and details of the operation are now being planned.

Cut to a shot of one of the men as he handles a model of the MIG-21. Closeup of the model in his hands. The camera holds on this closeup as the men talk. We learn that so many rubles have been budgeted for the operation. We learn that there will be two MIG-21s provided – one will be a backup plane. There will be the usual spare parts.

It has been decided, as a concession to the faction opposing Wilson, that all recent equipment will be removed from the planes. They will be repainted with North Vietnamese markings. We listen as personnel are discussed and agreed upon: there will be a maintenance officer, an armament man, and the necessary technicians and mechanics. The planning goes on, and the shot of the meeting gradually fades.

11

Three weeks later. Somewhere in the central part of the Soviet Union. Cut to a shot of a Soviet military vehicle – the red star is prominent – as it drives along an isolated road. The landscape is barren and semi-arid. In the background is a magnificent range of snow-capped mountains – possibly the Urals.

The camera shows the vehicle as it approaches the guarded entrance of an Air Force base. Aircraft hangars are visible in the distance. As the vehicle approaches the sentry gate, the camera shows four MIG-21s, making a formation takeoff, as they pass overhead at low altitude. We hear the incredible roar of the four jets.

Cut to a shot of the sentry gate. Two guards are standing there, armed with automatic rifles, watching the approach of the vehicle. The camera rises to show the sign mounted above the sentry gate. The sign contains the name of the Air Force base and also the name of the closest city: NOVOSIBIRSK.

Cut to a shot of the two men inside the vehicle. Wilson is in the passenger's seat. Everything is all set up now, and he has come to be checked out in the MIG-21. It will take several weeks of intensive training before he is thoroughly familiar with the aircraft.

Cut to a shot of the driver, who is a major in the Soviet Air Force. He is a good-looking man, a little younger than Wilson. We will see that he speaks English fluently and has been assigned to check Wilson out in the MIG-21. Later he will be his liaison in North Vietnam. The Major will be portrayed very favorably: the tough, dedicated communist, but also a warm-hearted man with a good sense of humor.

12

The next morning. The camera cuts to a rapid montage that shows various preparations for the flight training. We see Wilson in a doctor's office, his shirt off, getting a battery of innoculations for North Vietnam; the Russian Major, leaning against the wall, smiling as he observes the needle going in; Wilson having his eyes examined in another office; a closeup of his blinking eye through the opthalmologist's instrument; a quick shot of the eye-chart on the wall, with the Russian lettering.

Another rapid montage depicts the two MIG-21s being readied in one of the aircraft hangars. The camera shows them being repainted with North Vietnamese markings; a technician removing some of the electronic equipment; another technician gluing English names over the Russian names on the flight instruments. Some of the aircraft workers are women, and we hear them speaking in Russian to each other.

13

Two days later. The initial preparations are over and Wilson is ready to start flight training. Even for an experienced pilot, it still all begins in ground school. The camera cuts to the Russian Major as he begins to run a film for Wilson. We hear the *click* and *whirr* of the 16mm projector. Cut to the darkened screen as it is suddenly lighted, and the titles flash on in Russian.

The film-within-a-film begins. It appears to be one of the standard training films on the MIG-21, and the narration is in Russian. Cut to a shot of the Major as he turns the sound down – quick closeup of his fingers turning the knob – and begins to narrate the film in English.

Cut to a closeup of Wilson's attentive face, lighted from the screen. He watches the film and listens to the Major. We hear the *hum* of the projector, the sound of flickering film. Cut back to the screen. The film proceeds, the Major continues to narrate, and for a few seconds, before the fadeout, we all learn something about the MIG-21.

14

Three days later. The ground school phase is over and Wilson is ready to begin the actual flight training. Cut to a shot of the two MIG-21s parked on the flight line. The North Vietnamese markings are prominent. The two planes have been freshly painted and glisten in the sunshine.

Cut to a shot of Wilson and the Russian Major standing beside one of the MIGs. They are both dressed in flight gear. The camera cuts to a rapid montage that shows Wilson going through the standard pre-flight check of the aircraft. The Major walks along and observes. Shots of Wilson and the Major are intercut with shots of various parts of the aircraft as they are checked.

Cut to a shot of Wilson sitting in the cockpit. Another rapid montage shows him going through the standard cockpit check. The Major stands outside on the wing and observes as Wilson reads from a check-off list. Shots of Wilson and the Major are intercut with closeups of the various instruments and controls as they are checked.

The Major observes carefully as Wilson goes through the check-off list. At one point he interrupts and reaches into the cockpit and taps something on the instrument panel. Cut to Wilson as he looks up: he has made a mistake. The two men look at each other seriously for a moment and then grin broadly. It is evident that Wilson has been an excellent student and that the Major does not often get a chance to correct him.

Cut to a shot of the two men seated in the aircraft. Wilson is in the front seat, the Major is in the rear. The camera shows Wilson as he goes through the procedure of starting the engine for the first time. He speaks over the intercom to the Major, telling him every step of the starting procedure as it is performed. We hear the increasing whine of the jet turbine as it rotates faster and faster.

Cut to a shot of the MIG-21 as it taxis somewhere in the middle of the airfield. In the distance is the magnificent range of mountains. It is early December now and the peaks are covered with snow. The camera follows the plane as it turns at the end of the runway and is cleared for takeoff. We hear the rapid exchange of Russian between the Major and the control tower.

Cut to the gloved hand of the Major as he smoothly moves the throttle forward. We hear the sudden roar of the jet engine. Cut to a shot from the forward cockpit: the runway approaching faster and faster as the plane accelerates. We hear the Major speaking over the intercom to Wilson, telling him what he is doing, as he makes the takeoff.

The camera cuts to a closeup of the airspeed indicator as it reaches 115 knots. We hear the voice of the Major as he casually says, 'At 115 knots . . . we pull back on the stick.' Cut to a closeup of his gloved hand as he pulls back on the stick.

The camera shows the nosewheel of the MIG-21 as it lifts from the runway, then cuts to a shot of the entire plane as it leaves the ground. We hear the roar of the engine at full power. The landing gear retracts and the plane grows smaller in the distance as it gains speed and altitude. It passes over the end of the runway, climbs straight ahead for a few seconds, and then begins a climbing turn to the right.

The Major turns the controls over to Wilson when they are at altitude. Cut to a shot of Wilson as he takes the stick and begins to pilot a plane for the first time in four months. He puts the MIG into a gentle turn and then breaks into a broad smile. We can see that he is very happy to be flying again.

The camera cuts to a sequence of shots that depict the maneuvers of the first flight. The Major has Wilson go through the basics: climbing and descending turns, practice stalls, emergency procedures. They return to the airfield and make a few touch-and-go landings. Wilson quickly learns how to handle the Russian plane, and the Major is quite pleased. Towards the end of the flight they perform some simple acrobatics. They joke around – two pilots having fun in a high-performance aircraft.

15

Two weeks later. The training is completed except for one last flight. Cut to a shot of Wilson and the Major as they make a formation takeoff in the two MIG-21s. We hear the roar of the jet engines at full power. Shots of the takeoff are intercut with closeups of the two men in their cockpits.

Cut to a shot of the two MIGs flying in formation at high altitude. Closeups of the two pilots as they glance over at each other. The camera follows the two planes as they gracefully perform a series of acrobactic maneuvers: loops, barrel rolls, Immelmann turns.

There is a mock dogfight after the acrobatics, and Wilson manages to outmaneuver the Major. We see that he has become quite proficient in the MIG-21. The camera cuts to closeups of the two men in their cockpits, enjoying themselves immensely. There are aerial views of the striking location in central Asia – clouds, blue sky, snow-capped mountains.

PART
THREE

1

Hanoi, six weeks later. The scene is the darkened interior of a crowded moviehouse. The camera shows the agitated faces of the audience of North Vietnamese, illuminated by the light from the screen. They are shouting and chanting. Cut to the black-and-white newsreel that is showing: we see the faces of Johnson, Rusk, Bundy, and McNamera speaking before microphones at a press conference. We hear the shouting and chanting of the North Vietnamese.

Cut to a shot of the audience exiting into the crowded street. The camera then begins a rapid montage to give the sense of place, the feeling of Hanoi. Shots of the normal activities of the city are intermixed with shots of a nation at war. There are scenes of activities in shops, in the streets, at the markets, along the river. There are quick shots of scenes in parks, schools, offices, and factories.

The camera cuts to scenes of a nation at war – more specifically, a small country attempting to defend itself against aerial attack. We see a closeup of a radar screen, watched intently by a North Vietnamese girl; a shot of an anti-aircraft gun, manned by five soldiers; a shot of shells for the gun being unloaded and stacked by a team of men; a quick closeup of one of the shells, showing it to be Russian-made – the letters *CCCP*.

The scene shifts to an outlying district of Hanoi, an area that is almost rural. There is a quick shot of a sign by the roadside: it indicates that an airfield is nearby. The camera then cuts to a series of agricultural shots. We see farmers at work, chickens scratching in a yard, sows with litters of piglets, little boys on the backs of water buffaloes.

Cut to a shot of two Vietnamese peasants at work in a rice paddy. Closeups of their hands as they methodically plant rice in ankle-deep water. The camera holds on this shot, and we begin to hear a distinctive sound. It is the whine of a slow-flying jet coming in for a landing. It gradually becomes louder.

The two Vietnamese hear the sound and straighten up. Closeups of their faces as they shield their eyes and look towards the trees at the edge of the rice paddy. Cut to a shot of a MIG-21, with flaps and landing gear down, as it emerges from behind the trees and passes close overhead. It is Wilson returning from his eighteenth mission.

2

Ten seconds later. The camera shows the MIG-21 as it skims over the tropical vegetation at the end of the runway and makes a landing. Cut to a shot of Wilson as he brakes the plane. Quick closeup of his flight boots as they depress the pedals. He turns at the end of the runway and begins to taxi back to the parking area.

Cut to a tracking shot of the taxiing MIG-21. It is slightly distorted by the heat waves that shimmer above the sun-heated runway. We hear the whine of the jet engine. Palm trees and other tropical vegetation are visible in the background.

Cut to a closeup of Wilson's gloved hand as he pulls a lever in the cockpit. The hydraulically-operated canopy begins to slowly rise up. Cut to a shot of Wilson as he removes his flight helmet. We see that his face is already beginning to sweat in the tropical heat. He strips off his flight gloves, wipes his face on his sleeve, and puts on sunglasses.

The camera cuts to shots of various parts of the plane as it continues to taxi towards the parking area. There is a quick closeup of the nosewheel as it bounces over ridges in the concrete runway; a shot of the empty missile launchers beneath the wings; a closeup of the North Vietnamese markings on the rudder. The camera cuts back to Wilson in the cockpit, and then slowly moves down to the area below the canopy railing. We see the painted outlines of two American planes.

3

One minute later. Cut to the scene at the parking area. The taxiing MIG-21 is approaching – we can hear the sound of the engine – and a Vietnamese begins to guide it in with the customary hand signals. The camera shows the MIG as Wilson turns it with a combination of brake and throttle. He moves it forward until the Vietnamese holds up both palms in the STOP signal. Wilson halts the plane and immediately shuts down the engine. We hear the descending whine of the jet turbine as it slowly decreases in speed.

Cut to a shot of Wilson in the cockpit. He does various things on the instrument panel, unhitches his flight harness, collects some maps and other items, and then climbs out. It is evident that he has been through this post-mission routine many times. Wilson stands on the wing – we can see the sweat-patches on his flight suit – and makes a last check of the cockpit. Like all combat pilots he carries a service pistol. Quick closeup of the weapon – a Russian-made automatic.

The camera shows Wilson as he climbs down from the plane. Quick closeup of his flight boots as they finally touch solid ground – the asphalt of the parking area. We see that technicians and mechanics are already working on the plane. The camera cuts to quick shots of the various activities around a MIG-21 after a combat mission. We see men opening a panel to expose the ammunition reserve of the aerial cannon; dragging a fuel hose across the asphalt for the refueling; checking the air pressure in the tires; removing the exposed film from the gun cameras.

Wilson mentions a few things about the plane to the support personnel. We hear him speak in French with the Soviet maintenance officer, and also with the armament technician. There appears to be some trouble with one of the missile launchers, and Wilson points it out as he talks. Cut to a shot of the armament technician as he ducks under the wing to examine it.

The camera cuts back to Wilson as he stands beside his plane. He has a short exchange with the Vietnamese boy who is cleaning the splattered insects from the canopy. The boy grins broadly and Wilson smiles back. We see that he has picked up a few words of the language. Cut to a shot of a Vietnamese girl sitting on the wing, unscrewing the cap to the fuel tank. Wilson looks up and sees her, and there are quick closeups of their faces as they also exchange smiles.

4

One hour later. Wilson has debriefed, shed his sweat-soaked flight suit, taken a shower, and dressed in civilian clothes. We see him emerge from the Flight Operations Building into bright sunshine. He looks clean and cool, his hair is freshly combed, he is dressed in lightweight clothing for the tropics.

Tracking shot as he walks across a gravel driveway. Palm trees and tropical vegetation and bright-colored flowers are visible in the background. Suddenly there is the beep-beep of an automobile horn, and Wilson stops and looks around. Cut to a shot of a jeep-like military vehicle as it comes around the curve of the driveway. We see the Russian Major, who is Wilson's liaison in North Vietnam, behind the wheel.

The jeep-like vehicle comes to a halt – we hear the *scrunch* of gravel – and Wilson and the occupants of the jeep confront each other. The Russian Major and Wilson are smiling. They are good friends by now and are glad to see each other. The camaraderie of the two pilots is quite evident. The Major has even started to use American expressions in his exchanges with Wilson. We will hear that they sound a little funny with his Slavic accent.

Sitting beside the Major in the passenger seat of the jeep is an attractive young woman. The Major introduces her to Wilson – there are quick closeups of their smiling faces – and briefly gives the essentials of her background. She is French and has lived in Hanoi for several years. She writes for a Paris newspaper.

Wilson climbs into the back seat of the jeep and they drive off. He chats with the Major and the young woman as the jeep speeds along the narrow road. There is some talk about an interview for her newspaper. We can see that Wilson and the young woman already like each other. She asks him to call her Michele.

5

One hour later. The scene is a garden in a suburb of Hanoi. Palm trees and tropical vegetation and bright-colored flowers are in abundance. Visible in the background is a large house, a reminder of the years of French colonial rule. It is the kind of bourgeois setting that is really not supposed to exist in a socialist country.

The camera shows Wilson, Michele, and the Russian Major sitting around a garden table. They appear to be comfortable and relaxed and at ease. Tall drinks are on the table, and also several European newspapers with stories about Wilson. Cut to a closeup of a tape recorder resting on the grass. The reels are spinning, and we can see that the interview is in progress.

Cut to a shot of Michele. She is asking Wilson about the special circumstances of his role: an American pilot flying a Russian interceptor for the government of North Vietnam. Cut to Wilson. He explains some of the details of the arrangement, with occasional glances at the Major. We can see that some of the information is secret and not to be divulged, especially to a journalist. The Major shakes his head on several points. Wilson does say that his role is limited to the defense of the Hanoi area. He flies only to intercept attacking enemy aircraft.

Michele asks him whether the Russian MIG-21 or the American F-4 Phantom is the better aircraft. Wilson replies that he never flew the F-4, but that in his opinion they are both good planes. He tells her that he likes the relative simplicity of the MIG-21. There is less that can go wrong. He adds that all the equipment the Russians removed – he and the Major exchange smiles at this point – has made it very light, that it handles beautifully.

Michele asks him about the skill of the American pilots. Wilson replies that not only are the American planes very good, and the weapons systems excellent, but the pilots are well-trained and highly proficient. 'But most of them are young,' he adds. 'They haven't seen much combat.'

It turns out that Wilson downed his third American plane that day – an Air Force F-105 flying out of a base in Thailand. Michele asks him if the pilot was able to eject from the plane. Wilson says that he used an air-to-air missile and that the F-105 was almost totally destroyed. Michele is slightly moved and asks him how he feels. The Major listens gravely – he has never seen combat himself. Wilson is serious but detached and tells her about the impersonality of aerial combat.

Michele asks him if he has any curiosity about the identity of the American pilot. Wilson shakes his head. She persists and wonders aloud what kind of man he was. Wilson, accommodating her: 'I can give you a general image of the American pilots. This man was probably about twenty-five years old . . . he grew up in a small town . . . graduated from a state college . . . still goes to church . . . votes Republican . . . has a wife and child.' He looks impassively at the Major and Michele. 'He was probably quite a bit like me when I was in Korea.'

6

One week later. The scene shifts to an American aircraft carrier, located somewhere off the coast of North Vietnam. The opening shot is an aerial view of the carrier at sea. The camera then begins to move in. It moves in closer and closer until the men on the flight deck can be seen. It finally comes to hold on a Navy officer in a flight jacket as he walks along the deck.

Tracking shot of the officer as he passes various activities on the flight deck. We hear a mixture of shouted instructions, mechanical noises, jet engines being tested, the public address system. The camera cuts to quick shots of men working on aircraft. Aviation enthusiasts will recognize A-4 Skyhawks, F-4 Phantoms, A-7 Corsairs, RF-8 Crusaders, A-6 Intruders, RA-5 Vigilantes. Most of the planes bear Navy markings, but a Marine squadron is also attached to the carrier, and several planes are seen with the word MARINES painted on them.

The Navy officer continues his way along the flight deck. Cut to a closeup of the bright-colored squadron patch on his shoulder: two thunderbolts being dropped from the talons of a fierce-looking eagle. The camera rises to a closeup of his face. He looks as though he is in his late thirties. Cut to a closeup of the leather name tag on his flight jacket: R. D. RICHARDS/COM-MANDER/USN.

We will see that Commander Richards is the leader of one of the attack squadrons aboard the carrier. He is one of the principal characters in the film, even though he is not introduced until this point. Later we will learn that Wilson and the Commander were in the same squadron in Korea. They often flew together and were good friends. The Commander will be portrayed very favorably, more so than Professor Miller or the Russian Major or even Wilson himself.

7

One minute later. The camera shows Commander Richards as he opens a door and walks down a narrow passageway. He opens another door marked OPERA-TIONS and enters a room where a briefing is taking place. The camera cuts to the scene in the briefing room, and then cuts back to the Commander. He quietly takes a seat at the rear.

Cut to a shot of the intelligence officer at the front of the room. The camera holds on him for a few seconds and we listen to part of the briefing. The intelligence officer holds a pointer as he speaks. He occasionally indicates something on one of the maps and charts on display.

Cut to the scene in the briefing room. We see that about fifteen pilots are in attendance. It is not one of the pre-mission briefings, and the atmosphere is casual and relaxed. The camera cuts to closeups of the men as they listen and occasionally ask questions. We hear the knowledgeable replies of the intelligence officer.

Commander Richards takes over the briefing – the men are the pilots in his squadron – and begins the subject of aerial combat tactics. He uses a blackboard at first, then has the lights put out and begins a film. It is much better for depicting the relative positions of aircraft, the complicated three-dimensional maneuvers.

Commander Richards narrates the film-within-a-film as it runs. We all watch and listen, and for a few seconds we are all instructed in aerial combat tactics.

The Commander is heard to have a slight southern accent. He might be from a city in eastern Tennessee – Nashville, Knoxville, or Chattanooga – but he has lived in many places during his Navy career and the accent has diminished. His bearing and his manner of addressing his men indicates that he might be from an old family. His speech is that of a more educated man than is usual among Navy officers. He possibly attended the state university and then took a postgraduate degree at a private university in the East.

The film ends and the lights go on. Commander Richards takes up a different subject, one they have discussed before: the threat of the intercept missions flown by Wilson. We feel the mood in the briefing room become more somber. The camera cuts to a shot of an empty chair. It turns out that one pilot in the squadron, a man who was well-liked, is not present at the briefing. He was shot down by a lone MIG-21 the day before, and they think it was Wilson.

Commander Richards makes a reference to the wingman system that is used by American pilots. He tells his men that it is a proven system and is still their best defense against attacking MIGs. We listen as he quickly reviews the essentials of the system. He urges the pilots to stick to it and to always watch out for each other.

The camera cuts to one of the pilots. He asks Commander Richards if Wilson flies his intercept missions with a wingman. Cut back to the Commander as he shakes his head. He tells the pilot exactly what he has been told by the intelligence officer. Wilson occasionally flies with other North Vietnamese planes, but usually he goes up alone.

8

Twenty minutes later. The scene is a busy passageway somewhere on the carrier. The camera shows Navy officers and enlisted men as they pass in both directions. Cut to a quick shot of a door: we see the words OFFICERS LOUNGE. Cut back to the shot of the passageway. An officer in a flight jacket comes around the corner, looking at his watch. We see that it is Commander Richards.

Cut to a shot of two men inside the Officers Lounge. They are standing and talking together. One man is a civilian, dressed in a business suit, and the other is a Navy chaplain. Quick closeup of the little gold cross on his shirt collar. The camera shows the chaplain as he looks towards the door. He spots Commander Richards as he enters and calls to him.

Cut to a shot of the Commander as he hears the chaplain. He walks over to join the two men, and we listen as the chaplain makes the introduction. There is a quick closeup of the handshake. We learn that the man in the suit is an American journalist, and that he has an appointment with Commander Richards.

The chaplain excuses himself – he has to write a letter to the wife of a missing pilot – and Commander Richards and the journalist are left alone. They walk over to a quiet corner of the lounge where there is a table and two comfortable chairs. They sit down and are served coffee by a Filipino steward in a white jacket. They begin to talk.

The Commander quite naturally asks the journalist what magazine or newspaper he represents. Cut to a shot of the journalist as he begins to explain. He mentions magazines and newspapers he has worked for in the past. But this time, he explains, he is on assignment from a department in the Pentagon. It is one that handles public relations for the Navy.

After a few minutes the journalist happens to bring up the subject of Wilson, and the coverage of his exploits by the world press. He asks Commander Richards a few questions and the Commander answers them. The journalist asks if Wilson, as the renegade American pilot, has had a bad effect on morale. Cut to a shot of the Commander as he nods his head in agreement. He tells the journalist that his men feel very uneasy about Wilson.

The journalist: 'I understand you flew with Wilson in Korea.' Commander Richards: 'I did.' The journalist: 'Did you know him very well?' Commander Richards: 'We went through flight school together, and later we ended up in the same squadron. We were rather good friends.' The journalist asks if Wilson was a good pilot, and the Commander replies that he was one of the finest pilots in the squadron. He adds that Wilson was the only one to become an ace.

At this point Commander Richards takes a few minutes to explain the combat situation to the journalist. We listen as he describes the tactical advantages that Wilson enjoys. He is first of all flying a defensive role instead of an offensive one. He is flying over friendly territory while the U.S. pilots are over enemy territory. He has fuel tanks that are almost full, while the U.S. pilots have already used up a good portion of their supply.

Cut to a shot of the journalist as he rapidly writes in a notebook. Quick closeup of his pencil on the lined paper. He finishes writing and then asks whether the Russian MIG-21 or the American F-4 Phantom is the better aircraft. Cut back to Commander Richards. We listen to his voice – he is very much the professional military pilot – as he compares the two planes. He provides the journalist with the performance figures for both the F-4 and the MIG-21: rate of climb, cruising speed, ordnance load, combat ceiling, maximum range.

Commander Richards tells the journalist that the F-4 is considered to be superior to the MIG-21. But he goes on to explain that the tactical advantages Wilson enjoys make the difference. He adds, 'We carry a full load of bombs and air-to-ground rockets, which slow us down and are useless against Wilson. He carries only air-to-air missiles, which are relatively light.' The Commander mentions another factor: many of his men are right out of flight school, while Wilson is an experienced combat pilot. 'He has over 4,000 hours of flying time, most of it in fighters.'

Cut back to the journalist as he rapidly writes in his notebook. He finishes writing, looks up at the Commander, and then abruptly changes the subject. He begins to inquire about Wilson's personal life when he was in Korea. The journalist asks a number of questions, and Commander Richards is surprised at a few of them: whether Wilson drank very much, what he did when on leave in Japan, and so on. We can see that the Commander is annoyed by the way the journalist rephrases some of his answers. Nothing derogatory is revealed, however, and the journalist seems to be vaguely disappointed.

9

Cut to a shot of the Filipino steward in the white jacket as he approaches with a coffeepot. Closeup of his Oriental face as he refills the two cups. Quick closeup of the steaming coffee as it pours from the spout. The steward finishes pouring and then slowly walks away. The camera follows him, and in the background we can see the scene in the Officers Lounge.

Cut back to Commander Richards. He tells the journalist that it was 1962 when he volunteered for duty in Vietnam. He adds that he hasn't seen Wilson since then, almost five years ago. He looks at the journalist and says, 'You might say that Wilson and I have political differences.'

The journalist does not really ask, but seems quite willing to listen, and seems to be in full agreement, as Commander Richards explains why he volunteered for duty in Vietnam. 'China has got to be contained, or she will take over all of Southeast Asia. . . . No one who knows the history of China can deny that she is expansionist. . . . I hate the thought of the Vietnamese in those endless gray jackets. . . . We've got to fight somewhere, and it might as well be here. . . . We've got to *draw the line.*'

The Commander mentions these points and many more – all the arguments that the American people have been hearing for years. He delivers a strong defense of U.S. foreign policy in Southeast Asia. He is eloquent, sincere, and entirely convincing.

The public address system is heard – there is a quick shot of the squawk box – and Commander Richards looks at his watch. 'There's a mission due back in a few minutes. Let's go up on the bridge and watch them come in.' The two men get up and begin to leave the lounge. The public address system is heard again – we hear something about a doctor – and the Commander looks at the journalist and says, 'One of them has been hit.'

10

Cut to a distance shot of four F-4 Phantoms flying in a loose formation. The planes are over the open sea and are approaching the carrier. We hear the muted roar of the jet engines. The camera moves in closer to the formation until the word MARINES becomes visible on the four aircraft. The plane that has been hit is trailing a thin line of black smoke.

The carrier comes into sight in the distance, and the planes bank as they begin their approach and prepare to land. The camera cuts to shots of the gloved hand of a pilot as he performs various functions in the cockpit. We see shots of flaps being lowered, of landing gear coming down. There is a quick closeup of the light in the cockpit that tells the pilot his landing gear is down and locked.

Cut to a shot of the carrier deck. Everything is almost ready for the landings, and there is an atmosphere of controlled chaos as last-minute preparations are made. We hear the intermittent sound of the public address system. The camera cuts to shots of the various teams of men waiting at their stations. We see shots of other men hustling into position.

The first plane to land is the one which has been hit. It is seen coming in, low over the water, still trailing the thin line of black smoke. Cut to a shot of the flight deck officer as he speaks into a microphone. The pilot has been wounded and is being talked in.

Shots of the approaching plane are intercut with shots on the flight deck. There are closeups of the faces of the men as they watch the approach. We can feel the tense atmosphere aboard the carrier. Twice the Phantom begins to veer, but the correction is quickly made. The gradual approach of the plane lasts for a long time, perhaps one minute.

The camera shows the plane as it looms larger and larger at the end of the carrier deck. The muted roar of the engines is heard to increase. The Phantom seems to hang suspended above the stern, at the point of stalling, but then the wounded pilot cuts the throttle and the plane slams onto the deck and makes an arrested landing. Cut to a shot of the hook engaging one of the arrestor cables, and the cable stretching and holding the plane. Cut back to the plane as it comes to a halt and then rolls back a few feet.

The camera cuts to a rapid montage of shots. We see men performing various functions about the plane. There is a quick shot of a man releasing the cable and then lifting the arrestor hook back into position. Cut to a shot of a Navy doctor and a white-suited corpsman as they run across the deck towards the plane. The camera follows them until they reach the bullet-ridden cockpit. Cut to a shot of the cracked plexiglass of the canopy: behind it we can see the bloody pilot sagging forward in his flight harness.

11

Cut to an upper deck of the carrier. We see the journalist and Commander Richards standing together, looking down towards the flight deck. Their hands are on a steel railing, their hair is blowing in the wind. They have just observed the safe landing of the wounded pilot, and there is an atmosphere of relief.

Commander Richards makes an occasional remark to the journalist as the second and third Phantoms make routine landings. Shots of the two men are intercut with shots of the flight deck below. The word MARINES on the planes provokes the journalist to ask about the Marine squadron aboard the carrier. The Commander answers the question and then adds a humorous remark – in the tradition of the Navy – about the Marine Corps. Cut to closeups of both men as they smile.

They watch as the fourth plane – the leader of the flight – makes its approach and lands on the carrier deck. It is a routine landing like the two others. The plane slams onto the deck, is halted by the cable, and rolls back a few feet. The camera moves in slowly towards the cockpit area. Behind the plexiglass canopy the pilot can be vaguely seen as he performs various functions in his cockpit.

Cut to a closeup of the area directly below the canopy railing. The pilot's name and rank – First Lieutenant/

USMC – are seen stenciled in black paint. The camera then moves down to reveal what else is painted there: the outlines of three MIGs. The camera holds on the three MIGs for several seconds.

We hear the sound of the canopy being opened. The camera moves up and for the first time we see the face of the Marine Lieutenant. He is another one of the principal characters in the film, even though he is not introduced until this point.

The Marine Lieutenant has removed his flight helmet and has put on sunglasses. We see that he is unsmiling, that he has a lean and disciplined look. His sunglasses are the standard aviation sunglasses that are issued to all American pilots. The Marine Lieutenant is never seen without them.

Cut back to the upper deck of the carrier. The journalist is looking at the plane and seems to be somewhat excited. He tells Commander Richards that he has heard of that pilot in Washington and intends to interview him also. He asks the Commander several questions about the Marine Lieutenant and the Commander answers them. We learn that the Marine Lieutenant has shot down more MIGs than any other pilot on the carrier.

Cut to a shot of the Marine Lieutenant as he walks slowly away from his plane. He is stripping off his flight gloves. We see that the Marine Lieutenant has a lean build and is about six feet tall. He walks with the easy grace of an athlete. He has perfect posture and *looks* like a Marine.

We hear the voice of Commander Richards as he continues to talk to the journalist, providing him with some background and information on the Marine Lieutenant.

The Commander mentions that he has two probables in addition to the three MIGs. He tells the journalist that the Marine Lieutenant is a superb pilot, one of the finest he has ever seen.

Tracking shot of the Marine Lieutenant as he walks slowly past various activities on the flight deck. In the background we hear a mixture of shouted instructions, mechanical noises, the public address system. The camera cuts to shots of men working on aircraft. We see that some of them are watching the Marine Lieutenant as he walks. There is a quick shot of the journalist and Commander Richards looking down from above. The camera holds on the Marine Lieutenant as he walks slowly across the flight deck. We observe his unsmiling expression, his eyes hidden behind the sunglasses. This tracking shot lasts for a long time, and then dissolves into the next scene.

PART
FOUR

1

One week later. The scene shifts back to the airfield outside Hanoi. Wilson has just completed his twenty-ninth mission. He has debriefed, shed his flight suit, taken a shower, and dressed in civilian clothes. We see him emerge from the Flight Operations Building into bright sunshine. He looks clean and cool, his hair is freshly combed, he is dressed in his lightweight clothing for the tropics.

Tracking shot as he walks across the gravel driveway. The palm trees and tropical vegetation and bright-colored flowers are visible in the background. We hear the *scrunch* of his footsteps on the gravel. Cut to a closeup of his face. He sees someone he knows and smiles.

Cut to a shot of a ten-year-old sports car, parked in the shade of a palm tree. Michele is sitting behind the wheel. We see that she is wearing sunglasses and a blue scarf in her hair. The straps of her bra are faintly visible through her white blouse.

Cut back to Wilson as he comes up to the car and opens the door and gets in. He tosses a copy of *Le Monde* into the back and then leans over and gives her a kiss. The camera cuts to closeups of their faces. They are looking at each other, they are both smiling. All the signs are there, and we can see that a love affair is in progress.

Michele starts the engine of her car, shifts gears, and drives off. Tracking shot of the little car as it curves around the gravel driveway, the green tropical vegetation blurring in the background. They leave the airfield and turn onto the narrow road. We hear the sound of the car as it accelerates. They are off on an afternoon excursion.

As they drive along, the camera intercuts shots of present action – the two of them in the car – with shots of past action – a montage of scenes from the past two weeks. Shots of the present: the car speeding along the narrow road, scenes from along the roadside, shots of the two of them, closeups of Michele driving, closeups of Wilson.

Scenes from the past two weeks: Michele and Wilson looking down from the balcony of her apartment; having breakfast there a few minutes later; the two of them walking in the crowded streets of Hanoi; Michele pointing something out to Wilson as he looks in his French-Vietnamese dictionary; the two of them in the little bakery where she buys croissants 'as good as in Paris'; bumping into the Russian Major in the market, and being warmly greeted by him.

Additional scenes from the past two weeks: Michele taking Wilson through the zoological gardens in Hanoi; the two of them as they hand-feed one of the elephants; shots of some of the animals on exhibit that are native to Southeast Asia. The two of them having dinner with the Russian Major; Wilson opening the bottle of French wine; the portrait of Ho Chi Minh on the wall of the restaurant; Wilson opening a box of Cuban cigars; the Major showing snapshots of his wife and children.

Additional scenes from the past two weeks: Wilson

showing Michele around the airfield; the two of them watching a flight of MIG-21s during takeoff; Michele standing beside his parked MIG as he points something out; watching a Vietnamese as he paints the outline of the fourth American plane. The two of them out in the countryside, walking on a path alongside a rice paddy; watching two Vietnamese as they rhythmically plant rice; walking through the marketplace of a small village; watching a pretty Vietnamese girl as she rides past on a bicycle; purchasing a snack from a wrinkled old woman with a charcoal brazier.

The intercutting ends – the story of the past two weeks has been told – and there is a permanent return to present action. We see shots of the car speeding along the road, scenes from along the roadside, shots of the two of them, closeups of Michele driving, closeups of Wilson. The final shot in this sequence is of the car passing some little huts and rice paddies and then getting smaller and smaller in the distance.

2

Hanoi, three nights later. Cut to a shot of a motion-picture screen in a darkened room. Nothing else is visible, just the white screen. We hear a mixture of sounds: a quiet cough, the murmur of voices, a chair being moved. It is evident that a number of people are assembled.

An accented voice orders the film to begin. We hear the *click* and *whirr* of a 16mm projector being started, and then the sound of flickering film. The screen is suddenly lighted. Cut to a quick shot of the dust-filled stream of light from the projector: we see the dim outline of people around a conference table. Cut back to the screen to show numbers flashing and then the beginning of the film-within-a-film.

The people assembled around the conference table watch as the latest film from Wilson's gun cameras is shown. It is the record of his fifth American plane. A Navy A-4 Skyhawk is shown as it veers off to one side, a stream of tracer bullets pouring into it from Wilson's 30mm aerial cannon. We see the horizon appearing to tilt in the background at a steep angle. The bullets continue to pour into the Skyhawk for several seconds. Then black smoke begins to appear, the plane veers sharply, and it suddenly explodes.

The film abruptly ends. The projector is turned off,

the lights come on, and for the first time we see the people in the conference room. Most of them are in the military uniforms of the Soviet Union and North Vietnam. Several are smiling from the film. We see that one officer is in the uniform of the People's Republic of China. He wears rimless glasses and is not smiling.

Seated across the table from the Chinese officer is the only familiar face: the Russian Major. The camera holds on him as he gets to his feet and then moves slowly around the table. He goes to the projector and takes the reel of film from the Vietnamese projectionist. On his way back to his chair the Major stops to say something to the Chinese officer. The camera cuts to closeups of their faces as they look at each other. It is evident that they have met before and that there is antagonism between them.

Cut to a closeup of the expressionless face of the Chinese officer. The Major says quietly, 'At one time you said you would not trust him until he had shot down an American plane. Now he has shot down five, and you still do not trust him.' The Chinese officer says nothing. He and the Major look at each other – the repressed hostility is apparent – and then the Major walks away. The camera follows him as he returns to his chair on the other side of the conference table.

It becomes evident that this is a high-level meeting about Wilson. The discussion begins, and we learn that the Russians are delighted with the press coverage of Wilson's victories in the air. They consider the propaganda operation to be an unqualified success. But they are beginning to think about terminating the operation while it is still advantageous to do so.

The camera cuts to the faces of the participants as we listen to their voices. 'The propaganda operation is actually over . . . the objectives have already been achieved. . . . There is worldwide publicity. . . . We have many requests from pilots to fly in North Vietnam. . . . There are over twenty requests from France alone.' We listen to the various men. There is general agreement that the propaganda objectives have indeed been achieved.

The discussion now turns to the question of how to best terminate the operation. There is one obvious way. Cut to a closeup of the grave expression of the Russian Major – he did not expect this – as he listens to the Chinese officer talking about Wilson. 'Alive he is unpredictable and therefore dangerous. Dead he becomes a permanent hero, a martyr.' The Chinese officer continues: 'It would not be difficult. A simple device, actuated by an altimeter. . . .'

The meeting finally ends. The question of how and when to terminate the operation has not been resolved. It is agreed that they will meet again. The camera cuts to shots of the participants as they get up from their chairs. There are closeups of the faces of the Chinese officer and the Russian Major. They stonily regard each other across the conference table.

3

Two days later. A small village near Hanoi. Cut to a shot of a fifteen-year-old Vietnamese girl as she stands motionless in front of a hut. She blinks her eyes but does not move or change her expression. Several *clicks* from a camera are heard, and it becomes evident that she is posing for photographs. The girl is holding an ancient rifle in her hands.

Cut to a shot of Michele as she rapidly takes photographs with a 35mm camera. We see that she is standing in front of a large group of Vietnamese. They are talking among themselves and watching with great interest. Cut to a shot of the entire scene: we see Wilson standing off to one side in the background.

It turns out that Michele is working on a story for her newspaper. She had heard of the Vietnamese girl in Hanoi and has come to the village for an interview and some photographs. The girl has become somewhat famous throughout North Vietnam. There was a recent low-level attack by American planes, and a bullet from her rifle was responsible for bringing down an F-105 Thunderchief.

Michele takes her last photograph and then walks over to thank the girl. She talks with the girl for a few moments, making her smile, and then bids her goodbye in the Vietnamese manner and goes over to join Wilson.

She and Wilson begin to walk off. The camera follows them as they converse and move slowly through the streets of the village.

At one point they happen to see Vietnamese children coming out of a school. The camera holds on them for a few seconds and then cuts back to Wilson. We see that he has stopped walking and is staring at the children. Cut to a closeup of his face. The sequence that was seen earlier in Paris is repeated.

Wilson again seems to be slightly shaken. He looks at the children with that strange expression. The camera moves in to a closeup of his eyes. The sounds of the village fade away, and we begin to hear it again: the faint but increasing sound of a jet beginning a dive-bombing run.

The camera holds on the closeup of Wilson's staring eyes. The sound of the jet on the dive-bombing run steadily increases. When it has become quite loud, it is suddenly interrupted. We hear Michele's voice as she says something to Wilson, and the sound is no longer heard. Wilson is snapped away from his thoughts.

They turn a corner and the school is no longer in sight. The camera follows them as they walk up a little road that leads to the fields above the village. We see that the huts are beginning to thin out. After a few minutes they have left the village behind and are walking above it on a country road.

During this walk out of the village the camera occasionally cuts to closeups of their faces. They are engaged in a serious conversation. We listen as Michele tries to convince Wilson to stop flying. The Russian Major has secretly spoken with her, at great risk to himself, and has told her about the meeting. She has promised not to tell Wilson about it. They have agreed that Wilson's best chance is to stop flying before a decision is made to terminate the propaganda operation – which may involve sabotage of the MIG-21.

We see that Michele has just about convinced him to stop. He is listening carefully and knows that she is right. He knows that if he continues to fly he will eventually get killed, either by an accident or by the hand of an American pilot. He knows that aerial combat is ultimately a matter of probabilities, and that so far he has been lucky.

Michele describes their life together if he will stop flying. She makes it sound very attractive. They will live in Hanoi – she knows of an old French house that is available. He will teach at the university, where his skills and knowledge will be valuable to a developing country. They will be able to visit Paris twice a year. Michele goes on, and the camera cuts to a closeup of Wilson as he listens. He is almost convinced.

4

Cut to a shot of a Vietnamese woman as she runs along a path on the outskirts of the village. She runs until she reaches a large tree where a primitive alarm is positioned. It is a piece of steel plate suspended by two ropes. The woman picks up a club and begins to frantically strike the plate. The alarm sounds throughout the village, and the camera cuts to shots of the Vietnamese: they hear the alarm, become terrified, and hurry to take cover.

Cut back to Michele and Wilson as they walk along the country road. They hear the distant alarm from the village and stop walking. Cut to closeups of their faces as they look at each other. They both know what it means.

Suddenly they are hit by the incredible sound of the attacking American jet as it passes a few hundred feet overhead. They both dive into the ditch by the side of the road. The camera shows them as they lie there in the long grass and wait and listen. There are closeups of their tense faces. Then we hear it: from the direction of the village comes the sound of a powerful explosion.

After a few minutes Michele and Wilson get up out of the ditch and brush themselves off. They look at the sky but the plane seems to be gone. Cut to a column of black smoke rising from the village below. We can hear the sound of distant voices. Michele and Wilson take one more look at the sky and then begin to hurry down towards the village.

Cut to the scene in the section of the village that was hit by the bomb. There is smoke and confusion. Many people are running about. A bucket brigade, manned by Vietnamese of all ages, is extinguishing the fire in the building that was hit. The camera moves in as the flames are brought under control, and we see that the building is the school that was seen earlier. The roof is gone in most places and the building is an open shell. The camera continues to move in. The body of the first child is seen.

Cut to a shot of Michele and Wilson as they hurry down the road. They turn the corner and suddenly come upon the bombed school. They stop for a moment, horrified by what they see, and then continue towards the school. Tracking shot of the two of them as they pass the long line of Vietnamese manning the bucket brigade. They enter the burned-out shell of the building.

Cut to the scene inside the gutted school. The camera shows the last of the flames being extinguished by buckets of water. There is a quick shot of two Vietnamese hurrying past with an empty stretcher. Cut to a shot of Wilson as he suddenly sees the body of the child. Closeup of his stricken face.

After a few minutes Michele and Wilson are urged to leave the building by an old man with a long white beard. He is one of the village elders. The camera cuts to a closeup of his ancient face as he gently escorts them out. They leave the school and begin to walk down the street. We can see that Michele is almost in a state of shock.

They come to an area where the wounded children are

being treated. The camera cuts to a series of closeups, and we observe the medical treatment of the children. Michele and Wilson stand and watch. After a few minutes they walk on and come to another area where the little bodies are laid out in a line. The camera sweeps slowly from one end of the line to the other.

Michele finally breaks down. 'Why do they do it?' she cries, speaking of the American pilots. Cut to a closeup of Wilson. 'They don't know,' he says, speaking rapidly. 'They've got rockets and bombs to get rid of. They're in a hurry, they're being shot at. They've had buddies shot down.' Then Wilson looks at her and says, 'I did the same thing in Korea.'

5

Cut to a closeup of Michele as she looks at Wilson with disbelief. 'But you were a fighter pilot . . . you shot down five MIGs.' Cut back to Wilson. He tells her that he did more in Korea than shoot down those five MIGs. He tells her that like all fighter pilots, he also went on other missions – strafing and bombing missions.

The camera moves in to a closeup of Wilson as he begins to tell his story. After a few seconds there is a dissolve and the second flashback begins. The year is 1953. The scene is aboard an aircraft carrier off the coast of Korea.

Cut to a shot of Commander Richards. He is a lieutenant in this flashback and thirteen years younger. Richards is dressed in flight gear and has just returned from a mission. We listen as he tells Wilson how he strafed a building painted with crosses, supposedly a hospital, and how it blew sky-high. It was an ammunition dump disguised as a hospital.

One hour later. Cut to a briefing room aboard the carrier, and then to a shot of Wilson sitting in flight gear. He is a lieutenant j.g. in this flashback and also thirteen years younger. We observe a few seconds of the briefing. An intelligence officer displays an aerial-reconnaissance photograph of a school, and then goes on to explain that it is really a command post. Cut to a closeup of Wilson – he looks very young – as he sits and listens.

Two hours later. Cut to a shot of Wilson in the cockpit of his F2H Banshee as he makes a low-level attack on the command post. Closeup of his gloved hand squeezing the trigger on the stick. We hear the hammering noise of the 20mm aerial cannon, the *whoosh* of launching rockets.

Wilson completes the pass, pulls up, and begins his turn. He looks back at the target, and the camera cuts to a distance shot of the command post. We see that he has hit it squarely and it is burning. Cut back to Wilson as he prepares to make another pass. There was no anti-aircraft fire the first time, so he decides to fly in close before he launches his remaining rockets.

The camera shows Wilson as he lines up for his second pass at the command post. Closeup of his gloved hand as he pushes the stick forward, putting the Banshee into a gentle dive. We hear the faint but increasing sound of a jet on a dive-bombing run. After a few seconds we recognize the sound. It was heard before in Paris and in the village near Hanoi. It is the same sound that Wilson begins to hear whenever he sees children coming out of a school.

The camera cuts to closeups of his flight boots moving the rudder pedals, his gloved hands on the throttle and stick. The sound of the dive increases. Cut to a shot of the burning command post as it is seen through the forward canopy of the plane. It grows larger and larger on the screen.

The command post comes within range, and Wilson is about to open fire. The sound of the dive is at its maximum. Suddenly he sees children running from the blasted building, their clothes on fire. The intelligence was incorrect! The building actually *is* a school! Wilson passes low over the building, pulls up, and looks back. He is horrified at what he has seen, at what he has done.

The flashback ends and the camera dissolves back to the anguished face of Michele. She listens as Wilson completes his story. He has revealed to her what he has not been able to forget for the past thirteen years. It is the source of his deep feeling of guilt, the revelation of his primary motive for coming to North Vietnam. Now we know the reason for the repeated shots of Wilson looking at children coming out of schools.

PART
FIVE

1

Two days later. Cut to a shot of a two-man Bell helicopter flying over the open water. The dark shadow is seen below traveling rapidly over the waves. We hear the rapid bup-bup-bup of the rotors. The helicopter displays U.S. Navy markings. It is tilted forward and is flying at maximum speed. The camera cuts to a quick shot of the pilot at the controls – the sound of the rotors suddenly increases – and then cuts back to the shot of the helicopter as it proceeds.

Cut to a distance shot of the aircraft carrier as it steams somewhere off the coast of North Vietnam. The camera moves in to the area used for helicopter landings. A man is seen standing there, looking out over the water, and we begin to hear the faint but increasing sound of helicopter rotors. After a few seconds the man holds up his arms and begins to signal the helicopter in for a landing.

The shadow of the helicopter is seen first as it sweeps across the deck. Then the helicopter itself begins to come into view. The sound is louder but different as the pilot manipulates the pitch of the rotors for the landing. Cut to a shot of the man on the deck: his hair and clothing are whipped by the downdraft.

Cut back to the helicopter as it settles gently onto the deck. The sound of the rotors immediately begins to decrease. We see a small American flag on one of the landing skids. It indicates that the helicopter carries an officer of flag rank – in this case a rear admiral. The door of the helicopter opens, and the camera shows the Admiral as he steps out. We see that he is carrying a black attaché case. Cut to a quick closeup of the attaché case: printed on it are the words TOP SECRET.

Two hours later. Cut to the comfortable quarters of the Navy captain who is in command of the carrier. We see the Captain, Commander Richards, and the Admiral as they stand and talk together over a large desk. The attaché case marked TOP SECRET lies open. Quick closeup of what is also on the desk: a map of the Hanoi-Haiphong area of North Vietnam.

There is a knock on the door, and the Captain asks the caller to come in. The door opens and a Filipino steward in a white jacket enters. It is the same Filipino steward we saw earlier in the Officers Lounge. The steward walks over to a table, puts three empty glasses on a tray, and then looks over at the Captain. The Captain shakes his head, indicating that there will be no more drinks, and the steward turns and leaves.

The camera returns to the three men standing around the desk. It is evident that they have been talking for some time. Cut to closeups of their faces. The Admiral and the Captain look quite confident, but Commander Richards looks hesitant and worried.

It turns out that the rising toll of aircraft shot down by Wilson – and the attendent publicity – has forced the American government to act. There have been secret conferences in the Pentagon, the State Department, and the White House. Various courses of action have been discussed, numerous plans have been proposed.

At last one plan has been agreed upon. It has its risks and its disadvantages, but it is the one favored by the most influential advisors. It is also the course of action that the fewest people oppose. The decision has been made, and the machinery of the government has been set in motion. The three men aboard the carrier are the last links in the chain of command that will implement the plan.

The other two men have told Commander Richards about the plan and have discussed it with him in detail. He looks hesitant and worried for a number of reasons. The plan calls for the complete destruction – including all the buildings – of the airfield outside Hanoi. The method will be a surprise early-morning attack by four F-4 Phantoms from the carrier.

Cut to a closeup of a paper-clipped report lying on the desk. It is stamped TOP SECRET. Richards has already read it, but he picks it up anyway and looks through it again. It is the intelligence report on the airfield. Cut to a closeup of one of the pages. We see a map that shows the hangar where the two MIG-21s are sheltered. Richards turns the page, and there is a closeup of another map. It shows the building where the pilots are quartered. An 'X' marks the room occupied by Wilson. It is where he will be sleeping on the morning of the attack.

3

Commander Richards has already been talking with the two other men for some time. He has objected to the element of the plan that calls for the complete destruction of the buildings. Richards has mentioned the heavy loss of life that will be involved, the many Vietnamese that will be killed. He has not mentioned Wilson.

The intelligence report has also revealed that the Russian technicians are quartered at the airfield. Richards has mentioned this factor several times. He has asked if the killing of the Russians might not provoke some kind of counter-escalation.

Richards has quietly maintained – he is a commander in the presence of an admiral and a captain – that the destruction of the two MIG-21s would be sufficient to fulfill the objectives of the plan. He does not think the Russians would be likely to supply Wilson with two more aircraft.

The other two men have listened patiently to every point raised by the Commander. They have agreed with him that many of his objections are valid. But their answering argument is always the same. They maintain that the people in Washington who formulated the plan have a strategy and a perspective that is lacking aboard the carrier. They further maintain that the people in

Washington have access to more information, and are even more aware of the other considerations involved.

Richards is eventually overwhelmed by the two other men. He is overwhelmed by their rank, by what they represent, by their persistence, by the strain of the long meeting. He still objects to the plan, but is no longer able to oppose it.

The camera moves in towards the three men as they gather about the desk. Cut to the open map of the Hanoi-Haiphong area, and then to a quick closeup of the section that contains the airfield. The final details of the attack are agreed upon. We learn that the best pilots aboard the carrier, including the Marines, will be used. The rest of the Commander's squadron will be airborne to provide cover in case of a downed pilot. Cut to a closeup of the still-hesitant but defeated face of Commander Richards. The camera holds on this closeup as the Admiral schedules the attack for the following morning.

4

The next day, about an hour before sunrise. Cut to a shot from an upper deck of the carrier, looking towards the bow. The sky is beginning to be light in the east, and the flight deck is dimly visible. We hear the gentle sound of the waves lapping against the carrier. The camera holds on this opening shot for a long time, perhaps ten seconds.

Cut to one of the brightly-lighted areas below decks where the aircraft are readied for combat missions. Four F-4 Phantoms – two with Navy markings, two with Marine markings – are being worked on by a number of men. The camera cuts to a rapid montage, and we observe what is done to an F-4 before a combat mission. There are quick shots of fuel tanks being filled, tire pressures being checked, oxygen tanks being replaced. There are shots of ammunition being loaded for the aerial cannons, film being inserted into the gun cameras, bombs and rockets being affixed under the wings.

Cut to the map of the Hanoi-Haiphong area of North Vietnam. This time it is tacked to a display board instead of being unfolded on a desk. We hear the voice of a man giving weather information for the area. The unseen man is holding a pointer and indicating something on the map. Quick closeup of the tip of the pointer as it taps the section containing the airfield.

Cut to a shot of the entire scene. It is the same briefing room, the same intelligence officer, but this time the atmosphere is tense and the pilots are dressed in flight gear. The camera cuts to a quick closeup of one of the bright-colored squadron patches: the two thunderbolts being dropped from the talons of a fierce-looking eagle. There are closeups of the tense faces of several of the pilots.

Cut back to the shot of the briefing room. We see Commander Richards sitting at the rear. About fifteen pilots are attending the briefing, and all but two of them are Navy pilots from his squadron. The other two are Marines and are sitting together near the front.

The camera shows the intelligence officer as he concludes the weather part of the briefing. He repeats that there are patches of ground fog obscuring the target, but that they should be dissipated by the time of the attack. He looks at the clock – it is 5:15 a.m. – and then turns the briefing over to Commander Richards.

Cut to a tracking shot of the Commander as he gets to his feet and walks towards the front of the room. He passes the two Marines and the camera cuts to closeups of their faces. We see that one of them is the Marine Lieutenant.

5

Cut to a shot of a room in semi-darkness. The dim outlines of a bed and an overhead fan and tropical furniture can be seen. The camera cuts to a closeup of the luminous face of an alarm clock. We see that it is exactly 5:15a.m.

Cut to a shot of Wilson lying in bed. The camera begins to move in, and we see that his eyes are open. Wilson has been lying awake for some time, thinking of the school. The memory of the bombing is still fresh in his mind and he cannot sleep.

After a while he decides to get up. He throws back the covers and sits up on the edge of the bed. Cut to a closeup of the clock as he reaches over and pushes in the alarm with a *click*. It was set for seven o'clock – he is scheduled for a flight at nine. Wilson decides that since he has a morning flight he might as well get dressed in flight gear.

The camera cuts to a rapid montage that shows Wilson as he shaves, gets dressed, and leaves his room. He walks down the corridor – there is a quick closeup of the Russian Major's name on one of the doors – and emerges from the building. Tracking shot as he walks past tropical vegetation in the semi-darkness.

Wilson is on his way over to the Flight Operations Building to get some coffee. After a minute he reaches an open area between two patches of ground fog and stops walking. Cut to a closeup of his face as he stands and looks at the sky. He sees that it is beginning to be light in the east.

6

Twenty minutes later. Cut to the previous shot from the upper deck of the carrier, looking towards the bow. The flight deck below is clearly visible now in the early-morning light. It is filled with activity as pre-launch preparations take place. Men and equipment are seen moving across the deck. We hear a mixture of sounds: the distant voices of the men, various mechanical noises, the public address system.

Cut to a shot of four F-4 Phantoms parked at the rear of the flight deck. Their canopies are open. The pilots have just climbed in and are making their cockpit checks before putting on their flight helmets. The four jets are seen to be heavily loaded with bombs and rockets.

Cut to closeups of the four pilots as they make their cockpit checks. The Marine Lieutenant is shown first, then his wingman, and then Commander Richards. The camera holds on the fourth pilot, who is Commander Richards' wingman, for a longer time than the others. He is seen to be a lieutenant j.g. and the youngest of the four – perhaps twenty-three years old.

The pilots complete their cockpit preparations, put on their flight helmets, and begin to start their engines. We hear the increasing whine of the jet turbines as they rotate faster and faster. The camera cuts to closeups of all four pilots as they one-by-one give the 'thumbs up' signal. The first two Phantoms lower their canopies and begin to taxi towards the launching area.

Cut to an upper deck of the carrier. The Admiral and the Captain are seen standing together, their hands on a railing, as they observe the launch below. Cut back to the flight deck. We see the planes of Commander Richards and the young lieutenant j.g. as they move slowly towards the twin catapults of the launching area.

The camera shows the Commander's plane as it moves into position and is halted. Cut to a shot of the catapult mechanism below the plane: steam is seen emanating in several places. One of the catapult crew scrambles beneath the plane, attaches the catapult, and then quickly departs.

There are quick shots of the signals exchanged between the flight deck officer and Commander Richards. Then the camera cuts to the gloved hand of the Commander as he smoothly moves the throttle forward. Closeup of the instrument in the cockpit as it sweeps around to indicate full power. We hear the incredible roar of the twin jet engines.

Cut to a shot of Commander Richards as he gives the ready-to-launch signal. Cut back to the flight deck officer as he receives and acknowledges. There is a quick closeup of a finger pushing a button. We hear the *whoosh* of the steam-powered catapult, and the camera follows the heavily-loaded Phantom as it accelerates down the track. It leaves the carrier deck, drops a few feet, and then slowly begins to rise. We watch as the plane banks slightly and then begins a climbing turn to the right.

7

Cut to a closeup of a hand turning the keys in the ignition of a motor vehicle. We hear the sound of a cold engine turning over and then finally starting. Cut to a shot of Wilson behind the wheel of a jeep-like military vehicle. Closeup of his face as he revs the engine.

Cut to a shot of the jeep-like vehicle from ten feet away. The Flight Operations Building is seen in the background. It is partly hidden in the ground fog, which is rose-colored now from the rising sun. Cut back to Wilson. He looks out at the runway and sees that the ground fog is already beginning to burn off.

Wilson has just come from Flight Operations. He has had his coffee, looked over the weather maps, and filed a flight plan. He has told them he will go up now instead of at nine.

8

Ten minutes later. Cut to a shot of a small fishing boat as it drifts somewhere in the Gulf of Tonkin. It is lighted in the first rays of the rising sun and casts a long shadow over the water. We hear the cries of seagulls, the low voices of the unseen Vietnamese, the gentle lapping of the waves against the boat. The camera holds on this peaceful opening shot for a long time, perhaps ten seconds.

Suddenly there is an incredible roar as jet aircraft pass close overhead. The sound quickly diminishes, and the camera cuts to a shot of the four heavily-armed F-4 Phantoms. We see that they are flying in a tight formation at an extremely low altitude. The planes are bright in the early-morning sun.

The camera cuts to shots of the four pilots in their cockpits, and then holds on the Marine Lieutenant. We see closeups of his gloved hands on the stick and throttle, then a closeup of his impassive face. Cut to the area directly below the canopy railing. His name and rank – First Lieutenant/USMC – are once more seen stenciled in black paint. The camera moves down to show again the three MIGs.

Cut back to the shot of the four Phantoms in tight formation. The sunlight is gleaming on the plexiglass canopies and the polished aluminum surfaces. The camera moves in to show Commander Richards in the first plane. There is a quick closeup of his airspeed indicator as it quivers just below 600 knots. There is a closeup of his altimeter as it indicates 200 feet. The final shot in this sequence is from the cockpit of Commander Richards: through the forward part of his canopy we see the distant coast of North Vietnam.

9

Cut to a shot of long grass blowing in the breeze at the edge of a concrete runway. It is a repetition of the shot that opened the film. The camera holds on this shot and then slowly begins to rise until the red sun is seen. It is just above the trees on the horizon. Cut to a distance shot of the airfield. The buildings are seen in a low line about one-half mile away. The ground fog has completely burned off by now, and the buildings are bright in the early-morning sun.

Cut to a shot of the MIG-21 as it taxis somewhere between the buildings and the end of the runway. The plane is lighted in the first rays of the rising sun and casts a long shadow over the runway. We hear the steady whine of the jet engine. The canopy is seen to be open, and air-to-air missiles are visible beneath the wings. Below the canopy railing we see the painted outlines of the five American planes.

Cut back to the distance shot of the airfield from the end of the runway. This time the sound of the taxiing MIG-21 is heard as it approaches. The camera holds on this distance shot as the sound gradually increases, and the buildings are again seen in a low line about one-half mile away. After a few seconds the taxiing MIG-21 begins to come into view. We see the sunlight gleaming on the plexiglass canopy and the polished aluminum surfaces.

Cut to a shot of Wilson in the cockpit. He reaches the end of the runway and turns the plane with a combination of brake and throttle. He taxis forward a few feet and then applies the brakes and stops the plane. Wilson lowers his canopy and does a few things in the cockpit. Cut to a shot of the empty runway stretching ahead: we see that he is in position for takeoff.

10

Suddenly there is the sound of the first F-4 Phantom as it comes in at treetop level. The camera swings from the runway to the distant line of buildings, and Wilson watches as the first American plane streaks down the line. There is a flash and then the control tower explodes in flames. After a few seconds the sound of the explosion reaches his ears.

Wilson watches as the next three planes streak down the line of buildings. The aircraft hangars and his living quarters are hit. Black smoke billows into the sky, explosions rumble across the airfield. Wilson looks towards the line of burning buildings. Cut to a closeup of his face as he thinks of the Russian Major.

The fourth Phantom completes its bombing run and fades into the distance. Wilson knows the planes will come back for a second pass with rockets. He looks up at the sky and listens. Quick closeup of his watch as he makes himself wait for thirty seconds. When he is satisfied that there are only four planes, he moves his throttle forward.

Two minutes later. Cut to Commander Richards in the cockpit of the first Phantom. We see him streak over the trees at the edge of the airfield and make his second pass down the line of burning buildings. There are quick closeups of his gloved hand squeezing the trigger on the stick, quick shots of rockets being launched from beneath the wings. The Commander finishes his pass and begins to pull up.

Cut to a shot of his wingman, the young lieutenant j.g., who is following him in the second plane. He is calmly lining up for his second pass. The camera cuts to a closeup of his young face as he performs various functions in the cockpit. There is a closeup of his gloved hand as he moves it to the instrument panel. He flicks the firing switch from BOMBS to ROCKETS.

Suddenly there is a rapid metallic noise, and the Phantom shudders as it is hit by ground fire. Cut to a quick shot of the fuselage: bullet holes can be seen. We hear the decreasing sound of the jet engines as they begin to lose power. Cut to a closeup of the young lieutenant j.g. as he realizes he is hit. He struggles to control the plane.

The camera cuts to the instrument in the cockpit that indicates power. We see that it is rapidly falling off. Cut back to the young pilot as he pulls back on the stick to maintain altitude. He looks out both sides of the canopy, and the camera cuts to shots of the jungle below.

The lieutenant j.g. prepares to eject. We listen as he gets off a quick radio message, telling the others he has been hit by ground fire. He gives his position and tells them he is about to eject. The camera then begins a rapid montage that shows the action of the next two minutes in a matter of seconds.

We see the lieutenant j.g. as he activates the ejection mechanism; the pilot, seat, and canopy blasting up from the plane; the parachute opening and the pilot floating down; the disabled plane crashing into the jungle and exploding; the pilot landing in a clearing, unhitching his parachute, and quickly heading into the jungle.

12

Cut to a shot of Wilson in his cockpit. He has by this time gained speed and altitude following his takeoff. Wilson knows the first plane will be flying low and slow as it comes off the airfield after the pass with rockets. He has planned his attack and is in position high above the airfield.

Wilson looks out the side of his canopy. He spots the first Phantom coming off the airfield, and the camera cuts to a distance shot. We see a tiny glint of metal as the plane passes from the airfield to the bordering jungle. Cut back to Wilson. He glances coolly down and waits for the right moment.

Cut to Commander Richards in the first Phantom as he climbs away from the airfield. He looks back over his shoulder, and the camera cuts to a shot of the burning buildings in the distance. The Commander has just heard the radio message from the lieutenant j.g. He knows that he is no longer covered by a wingman.

The Commander climbs away from the airfield for about ten seconds and then begins his turn. Cut to a shot of Wilson as he watches from above. When he sees the direction of the turn, he immediately begins his attack. Closeup of his gloved hand as he swiftly moves the stick to the right.

The camera cuts to a shot of the MIG-21 against a

background of white clouds and blue sky. It smoothly rotates into a vertical bank, and we watch one of the classic shots of aerial combat: the attacking plane in a sideslip as it begins to drop towards the target. After a few seconds the horizon comes into view and then the green jungle far below.

Wilson swiftly closes in within range and fires one of his air-to-air missiles. There is a shot of the missile being launched from beneath the wing and then tracking towards the Commander's plane. Richards is alerted by his radar. We see a closeup of the rapidly-approaching blip on his radar screen. He takes evasive action, but the missile explodes close enough to cause severe damage.

The camera shows smoke beginning to trail from the fuselage of the crippled Phantom. Cut to a closeup of the Commander – there is smoke in the cockpit – as he attempts to control the plane. We listen as he gets off a quick radio message. He warns the Marine Lieutenant and his wingman about the attacking MIG.

Richards is about to eject when a second missile launched by Wilson scores a direct hit. The plane explodes and the Commander is killed. Cut to a closeup of Wilson as he looks down from his cockpit. He watches the wreckage of the Phantom during its long smoke-trailing plunge to the jungle below.

13

The Marine Lieutenant, who is lining up for his rocket run, has heard the Commander's warning over the radio. Cut to a closeup of his impassive face as he receives the message. He immediately breaks off his rocket run and jettisons his remaining bombs and rockets. There is a quick shot of them falling away from beneath the wings. Cut to a closeup of his gloved hand on the throttle. He puts the Phantom into afterburner.

14

In the aerial battle that follows, the clouds and the jungle horizon are seen to tilt at all angles as Wilson and the Marine Lieutenant maneuver for position. Closeups of the two pilots in their cockpits are intercut with shots of the two planes as they climb and bank and dive. Wilson pilots the MIG-21 with great skill, but this time the odds are on the side of the Marine Lieutenant. He is the younger man, he is flying the superior plane, and he is covered at all times by his wingman.

After much maneuvering, the Marine Lieutenant at last gets into position behind Wilson. He closes in within range and opens fire with his aerial cannon. Cut to a closeup of his gloved hand squeezing the trigger on the stick. Closeup of his face as he fires. We hear the hammering noise of the aerial cannon.

The camera shows the MIG-21 as it veers off to one side, a stream of tracer bullets pouring into it. The horizon appears to tilt in the background at a steep angle. We watch as the bullets continue to pour into the MIG for several seconds. Then black smoke begins to appear, the plane veers sharply, and it suddenly explodes.

Cut to a closeup of the Marine Lieutenant as he looks down from his cockpit. He watches the wreckage of the MIG during its long smoke-trailing plunge to the jungle below. It happens to crash not far from the burning wreckage of Commander Richards' plane.

The Marine Lieutenant is joined by his wingman and they survey the scene below. Cut to a shot of the two American planes in tight formation: we see the word MARINES in big letters. The final shot in the film is from the cockpit of the Marine Lieutenant. He has the plane in a gentle bank, and from the side of his canopy is an aerial view of the scene below. The camera holds for a long time on the final shot: two columns of black smoke rising from the green jungle.